Into the Evermore

The Gentry of Paradise

Holly Bush

HOLLY BUSH BOOKS

Copyright © 2017 Holly Bush

All rights reserved. No part of this publication may be reproduced, distributed, or transmitted in any form or by any means, including photocopying, recording, or other electronic or mechanical methods, without the prior written permission of the publisher, except in the case of brief quotations embodied in critical reviews and certain other noncommercial uses permitted by copyright law.

Heartfelt thanks to Hollie Shirey McDowell for sharing her equine expertise with a novice.

Chapter One

November 1842 Virginia

"Twenty dollars and you can have her. Don't make no never mind to me what you do with her. I just want to see the gold first."

The filthy-looking bearded man waved his gun in every direction as he spoke, including at the head of the young woman he held in his arms and at the three men in front of him. The trio all had handkerchiefs covering the lower part of their faces and hats pulled down tight, revealing six eyes now riveted to the pistol as it honed in on one random target after the other. The woman was struggling, although it was a pitiful attempt as she was clearly exhausted, and maybe hurt. The wind whipped through the trees, blowing the dry snow in circles around them. Beau Gentry watched the grim scene play out as he peered around a boulder down into a small ravine. He'd been propped against the sheltered rock, dozing, and thinking he'd best start a fire, when he heard voices below.

"Ain't paying twenty dollars in gold for some used-up whore," one of the masked men said.

The filthy man wrenched his arm tighter around the woman and put the gun to her temple. "Tell 'em, girly. Tell 'em you ain't no whore."

She shrank away from the barrel of the gun and moaned. "Please, mister. Let me go," she begged.

"Tell 'em you ain't no whore!"

She shook her head and pulled at the filthy man's arm around her waist. "I'm no fallen lady," she whispered. "I'm just, I'm just . . ." The woman went limp, and Beau thought she'd fainted but instead she vomited into the snow in front of her. He watched her choke and gag, bent over the man's arm, and that's when he realized she was barefoot.

Beau leaned back against the rock and checked his pistols and shotgun beside him. He hoped his horse wouldn't bolt from the tree she was loosely tied to when the bullets started to fly. It'd be a long walk back to Winchester if she did, especially as he'd most likely be carrying the woman. "Shit," he muttered. "Shit and damnation. She doesn't have any goddamn shoes on."

From his angle, he'd need to drop the three bandits with the two shells from the shotgun, and finish off any of them still breathing with one of his pistols. They'd be surprised and hopefully slow if the liquor smell floating on the wind meant anything. He was counting on the filthy man being hampered by the woman's struggling. He was hoping she didn't get shot in the cross fire, but then she'd be better off dead than facing what was in store for her if the filthy man was the victor. The argument over the gold was getting heated, he could hear, making this as good a time as any.

The snow fell away from the fur collar and trim of Beau's coat as he stood, lifted the shotgun to his shoulder, and aimed at the first man. He pulled the trigger, sighted in the second man, and pulled the second trigger right after the other, marching forward through brush and snow, letting the shotgun fall from his hands as he went. Two of the men dropped and the third fell to his knees, aiming his pistol at Beau as he did. Beau lengthened his stride, pulled a pistol from his waistband as he made the clearing, raised his left arm straight, and dropped the kneeling man to the ground with a shot to his face, letting the spent weapon fall to the ground. As he turned, he pulled his new fighting knife free of its scabbard and brought his right hand up, wielding a second pistol, side-stepping to get an angle on the filthy man.

"She's mine! You ain't getting her."

"Drop the gun."

"Twenty dollars in gold and you can have her!"

He wondered how much longer the woman would last. She was white-faced, except for the dirt, and her hair hung in clumps, matted together with blood. Her mouth was open in a silent scream. She raised and lowered her arms as if paddling in a pool of water. Most likely she was long past terrified and all the way to hysterical.

"Fine," Beau said. "You want twenty dollars?"

The filthy man nodded, and Beau dropped his knife in the snow and reached his hand in his pants pocket as if intending to retrieve a gold piece. The man lowered his weapon by an inch or so as his eyes followed Beau's hand, and in that moment Beau brought up his right hand and fired his weapon. The bullet tore through the man's neck, sending blood gushing into the snow as the man tumbled sideways, releasing the woman. She fell in the opposite direction, covered in splattered blood, clawing and crawling away from her captor, turning on her back and shoving off in the mud and snow with bleeding feet, pushing herself away. Her cry echoed in the silent cold night.

Beau pulled his knife from the snow, kicked away the filthy man's gun, and walked to where he lay, now writhing as he slowly drowned in his own blood. The hair on the back of Beau's neck stood and he turned. The last of the three men, missing part of his cheek and ear, had retrieved a loaded pistol from the belt of one of his companions and was now aiming it at Beau with shaking hands. Beau released the knife with a whip of his wrist, landing it dead center on the man's chest. He turned to the woman and watched as her eyes rolled back in her head and she crumbled the last four or five inches, until her back hit the forest floor.

Eleanor awoke suddenly, her eyes opening fully, having no idea where she was, or the time of day, or even what day it was. Panic hit her as she felt the weight of something over her body. Danger and death had hung over her since... that day, since everything dear and known was taken from her. Had she been *sold*? She took a deep breath and tried to wrap her mind around the reality of it, around the fact that she was someone's property, rather than a living, thinking person on her own.

She sniffed the air and her nose was tickled by

fur. It was then she realized the weight she felt was furs or blankets, tucked around her tightly, up to her chin. Could she be warm? Her head pounded a slow beat in her ears, and any movement exaggerated the ache. Her feet were burning as if she were stepping on coals. She noticed a fireplace with a roaring fire on the other side of the small room. And there was a person, a man, kneeling in front of the fire, poking it and adding logs as he did. Who was he? Her thoughts were muddled and her memory as random as the sparks shooting from the new wood. He turned then and looked at her.

Her hands fought their way out from under the heavy robes and she shrieked. Every muscle and bone in her body prepared to defend itself from whatever new danger he presented. She knew she was moving much too slowly, but she couldn't squeeze one more bit of energy to even prop herself up, if not climb out of the bed and run for her life.

"Shhh," he said without standing or making any movement. "Steady, now. I'm not going to hurt you."

Eleanor was taking in short breaths and she could feel her heart racing. Tears came to her eyes as she thought about her own death, hopefully quick, as her mother's had not been. She was ready to meet her maker and be reunited with her family. She had lived a good and dutiful life, and she was lucky, she knew, to be the daughter of Gordon and Olivia McManus, but now she longed for peace, for her savior's grace that would heal her suffering and fill her fearful heart with calm.

She watched the man stretch out to his full height, turn, and seat himself in a chair near the fire. He rocked slowly, back and forth, back and forth. He had both hands on the arms of the chair and his feet firmly planted on the floor. He wasn't even looking at her; in fact, his eyes were drifting shut.

"Who are you?" she whispered.

"Beauregard Gentry. Originally from Concordia Parish, Louisiana. Left there five years ago with an uncle to help him with a lumber mill left to him by his wife's side of the family after her and her parents' death. The business was contested by a distant relative, and Uncle Chester and I decided to head to Canada to try our hand at the fur business. He took a chill six months past and died."

Eleanor listened intently as his accent was unique to her ears. She got the feeling he was telling the story for her benefit, to calm her. He returned to rocking when he was finished, back and forth, back and forth. She was staring at him, and he turned his head to her.

"Would you like some water? Are you thirsty?"

She nodded.

"I'm going to stand now and fill that cup there from the bucket. I'm going to set it down near your bed. Do you think you can drink it yourself?"

She nodded again, eyes glued to him as he slowly stood and walked to the dry sink. He poured water in a wooden cup and turned. She was suddenly parched, as if his mention of water made her mind connect with the needs of her body. He walked around the edge of the room, away from her until he came to the table near her bed. He sat the glass down and slid it to her with one finger. He backed up and sat down in the chair.

She pushed herself up on her elbows and licked her lips. She touched the cup with a trembling hand and concentrated on gripping it without spilling its contents. She drank greedily. She sat it down on the table and lay back on the pillow, pulling the warm blankets up to her chin. She could not stop the tear that fell down her temple and into her hair.

"What are you going to do with me?" she asked.

"I'm going to take you wherever you need to go."

Eleanor shook her head, staring at the wood ceiling as she did. "There's nowhere for me to go."

"There's got to be somewhere for you to go.

Shit, there's somewhere for everybody to go."

"No. There is nowhere for me," she whispered and closed her eyes.

* * *

Beau chopped wood and shot squirrels and rabbits 'til he had enough firewood for the following winter and enough raggedy-ass pelts to make a sleeve of a coat. It was the third day since he took the woman to the deserted cabin he'd seen as he started the long trip carrying her and leading the horse and mule back to Winchester. He stuffed the holes in the walls with rags and built a fire he kept burning night and day. He looked up at the gray sky, now promising to drop another coating of snow, and hoped the lean-to he'd pitched would be enough to keep his horse and pack mule dry and warm 'til he could get the woman back to civilization. *Then* he could find the property named on the deed his uncle had given him before he died.

He unhooked the rope from the door and hurried inside before the heat let out and the woman began shivering like she had the day before. But before he hung his hat on the peg near the door, he saw her standing by the fire, her back to the stone mantel.

"You're awake."

She nodded.

"I'm just going to set this firewood down," he said and walked near the fireplace and stacked the wood on the pile near the hearth.

Beau kept his eyes straight ahead, knowing she watched his every move. He shrugged out of his coat when he was done, hung it next to his hat, and leaned back against the wall, giving her as much space as he could.

"How long?" she asked.

"Three days."

"What do you mean to do with me?"

He shook his head. "Don't aim to do a damn thing *with* you. Winchester's the closest town. I plan to take you there. You can find your people or do whatever you were doing before I found you out here in the wilderness."

"I can't. I can never do what I was doing before."

"Are you from around these parts, miss?"

"Pennsylvania."

"Then you're a long way from home."

She nodded and looked away from him and flinched as if someone had touched her shoulder and frightened her.

He was quiet for a long minute, hoping she'd reveal something of herself, but she stood silently staring at the wall.

"I found a barrel yesterday 'round back of the cabin. I thought you might want to clean up a bit," he said. "I'll bucket you some water from the stream to the kettle on the hearth, and we can fill the barrel with warm water. I'll take myself off some other damn place and give you some privacy."

She turned her head sharply. "How would I know you won't come back in?"

Beau shrugged. "'Cause I said I wouldn't, and I keep my word. My mother would have beat my ass end with a switch if I didn't."

Beau left to fill the buckets and haul the barrel. She stood watching him, in the door and out, her back to the hearth. He dumped the last heated kettle of warm water and looked up at her. She was staring at him with the bland expression she'd worn before, as if she was incapable of any happiness or sadness.

"Are you going to use any of this water or just stand there and look at it?" he asked.

Her eyes flitted to the door.

"I'm going to drag this table over here," he said and inched the furniture. "When I leave, you push it up against the door. Are you strong enough?"

She watched him and nodded. He went out the door and waited until he heard the scrape of wood on wood. "Do you have it tight against the door?" he shouted.

"Yes," he barely heard and then, "Yes."

Even with the sun shining, he was starting to get cold and he certainly was bored, after what he figured was well past the second hour standing outside. He rode his horse around a small clearing near the cabin, and he figured he was probably as happy to do it as his horse was since they'd both been doing nothing for three days. He brushed the nag and checked her hooves before feeding her what he'd gathered.

The door to the cabin opened and stood ajar, although the woman did not come out. He kicked the mud off of his boots and went inside. She was bent over, stirring the stewpot hooked in the back of the fireplace, and straightened as he came in. "I'll get the water dumped for—" he said, stopping as she turned to him.

Her long hair was damp but already shiny and reflecting a deep red in the light of the fireplace. She had the greenest eyes he'd ever seen on a person, and a smattering of light freckles across her nose and cheeks that he'd not noticed before she cleaned up. At that moment he decided she was as pretty a young woman as he'd ever seen. He took off his hat. "I'll take care of the water, miss."

She shook her head and pointed near the dry sink. "I found a pull that opens the floor to the ground. Much of it splashed out as I washed my laundry but I bucketed the rest of it down the opening. I can't budge the barrel, though. You'll have to take care of that."

Beau nodded and pulled and pushed the barrel out the door, dumped the remaining water, and stood it against the cabin in the back. He wiped his hand down his beard and over his brow and thought he might have to do something about cleaning himself up, especially now that this young woman was looking like she was from a good family and on her way to a social or a church picnic. He'd get his kit and at least shave. It was then he wondered what she'd used for soap as he'd not offered the sliver he carried.

Beau came back in the cabin and nodded to the pot she stirred. "It's just some rabbit I'm stewing there with two potatoes I've been carrying in my saddlebag. Help yourself. You must be hungry as blazes if you're feeling better."

"It smells wonderful, Mr. Gentry. Thank you. I am hungry. May I dip you some?"

"I already ate, but you go right ahead, miss."

She turned to the fireplace, stopped short of reaching for the long-handled ladle, and turned back to him. "Eleanor McManus. My name is Eleanor McManus."

"It's a pleasure to make your acquaintance, Miss Eleanor."

"I must thank you for all you have done for me, Mr. Gentry." She swallowed and folded her hands at her waist. "I could never repay it. Not in a thousand years."

"So you believe me when I say I'm just going to take you to Winchester? To your people?"

"I do believe you. You would not have brought me to this cabin and kept me warm and dry and let me heal. You would not have rescued my mother's valise from the snow and bothered to bring it for me. You would not have..." she trailed off and looked out the lone window of the cabin. "You would not have been so careful to edge around the room so that I would not be frightened."

"You've been through a hellish ordeal by my reckoning."

"And you have gone out of your way for me," Eleanor said. Not true of others and especially of one person. Was it a sin to feel as badly as she did over a broken heart as she did over the death of her parents and sisters? Would she burn in hell? She thought perhaps she would. Tears came to her eyes as the image of her family swam before her. All gone. All in the hands of the Lord.

"Nothing more than anyone else would do," he said.

She shook her head. "No. You're so very wrong about that."

Eleanor turned to the fireplace, suddenly starved and weak-kneed from it. She ladled pieces of meat, broth, and potato into the tin plate that had been propped up on the mantel. She sat down on the edge of the bed, and he handed her a spoon. The meat was tender and delicious. She ate slowly, knowing that too much food on a stomach that had been nearly empty for some days would be calamitous.

Mr. Gentry still stood near the dry sink as he'd been doing since he came in. It was just then she realized he hadn't sat down in the rocker because she had clothes, even unmentionables, hanging from the chair in the heat from the fireplace. She stood and gathered them all in her arms.

"Please sit down. You've been on your feet all day so I could wash. Please sit."

"You did some laundry I see."

"Yes. It was such a gift to get the smell of blood and dirt and grime from my person, and to clean my clothes. This dress," she said with a catch in her throat, "was my mother's. That horrible man grabbed her valise from the wagon when he took me."

"Can you tell me what happened?"

"We were traveling from Allentown, Pennsylvania,

with a group of families, planning on settling near Charleston, Virginia, where my father had a connection. He was a minister, you see, and he intended to build a church there. We were separated from the rest of the group because of a broken axle on our wagon. My father felt we would be able to catch up with the others in less than a week as he had mapped out our directions with stops along the way, in towns or with families he knew through the church. We were more than halfway on our journey and using well-traveled roads."

She stopped, feeling the tears spill over onto her cheeks. "They came in the middle of the night and shot Father and my two sisters immediately. Mother screamed 'run' and I did, and for whatever reason, they did not follow me, but I stopped, foolishly. I had to see. That was when I saw them tearing her clothes off of her body. The last thing I heard was her screams."

Eleanor did not know how long she sat staring, the image of her father's body, twisted and bloody, and her mother standing naked, trying desperately to cover herself. She did not know if she would ever get the image out of her head. Mr. Gentry cleared his throat and stood to throw a log on the fire.

"You got away?"

"We'd been in Winchester for a week or more,

resting the horses and getting our wagon fixed. I ran and ran until I found my way back to town. I went to the church that we'd attended while there for help from one of the congregants and they gave me clothes as I was still in my nightdress and they fed me. I asked them to post a letter for me to my father's sister, my only living relative, that he'd been killed. Perhaps I should have asked to borrow money to get myself back to Allentown and then find a way to my aunt in Philadelphia. I admit I wasn't thinking straight. I begged for help from . . ."

Eleanor stood, unable to divulge the final dagger to her heart. "I went back to our wagons the following day to bury my parents and retrieve what I could, and that horrible, filthy man came out of the trees and grabbed me. We rode from morning until night, in circles I think, my hands tied to the saddle horn. I thought for certain I was to die when I saw you come out of the woods and kill those men. But then I'd been anticipating my own death for several days at that point."

Eleanor lay down on the bed and pulled the covers up to her chin. Mr. Gentry sang a song she'd never heard, and then hummed the melody for some time. She let herself drift off to sleep, dry and clean and nearly free of fear.

Chapter Two

"I think it's time we get you to Winchester," Beau said the following morning.

He had cleaned up the area, buried the garbage and waste, and strapped his furs over the back end of his pack mule and helped Eleanor get herself settled on the animal. He cinched down her valise and lead the mule and his horse through the brush and bramble. They came upon a well-traveled path and began seeing others. He kept his hand on his pistol as he nodded to passersby. The woman sat still, eyes downward, and made no response to the occasional halloos.

Early in the afternoon, Winchester came into view as they rode out of the foothills and into the streets of the city. "I'll deliver you where you need to go, miss."

She slipped down the mule's side and looked up at him. "Thank you, Mr. Gentry, for everything you've done. For all the kindnesses you've shown me, which are many. You are a good man, sir. I wish you luck."

"What the hell's the matter with you?" he whispered as he dismounted, holding the reins for his horse and the mule. "We're right in the middle of all the saloons. I can't leave you here. You said that your father knew people in the towns you stopped in. Who did you socialize with here? Where's that church you ran to that night?"

"There's no one," she said and turned, walking slowly through the wet street, pulling a shawl tight around her shoulders and carrying her mother's bag.

"Miss! I can't just leave you here in this Sodom and Gomorrah."

She turned with the shadow of a smile, the first he'd seen from her. "Thank you, Mr. Gentry. I must find my way on my own. There is no use putting it off."

Beau watched her walk down the wood planks in front of the saloons, her head bowed. A few men whistled and bent over in mock bows but most stepped aside for her. He mounted his horse and followed her at some distance down streets, and up avenues, until she came to a church. She stood motionless in front of it, staring up at the steeple, as if getting her bearings and maybe gathering courage, although why anyone would need courage to enter a church, he could not begin to imagine. He tied up the horse and mule and leaned against the post, wondering why he cared. Why was he still even standing there? He'd rescued her, kept her warm and safe until she healed, and now delivered her to people who would be familiar to her. Church people like her parents and the others on their wagon train.

Even as he wondered why he was still there, his feet took him on a well-worn rock path along the side of the building. He stopped when he heard voices but glanced around the corner to see a grassy area with the last of the fall trees in a blaze of color, around benches and wooden chairs. She was seated on one of the benches, speaking to an older gray-haired man wearing a collar of the church. There was a younger man standing, tapping his foot, holding his hat behind his back, and staring at Miss McManus as she spoke with the older man.

"I have one elderly aunt in Philadelphia, my father's sister, who was quite ill when we left. She may have already passed on to her reward by now."

"There won't be anyone from our flock traveling to Charleston until spring at the earliest. Do you have aunts or uncles or other family already there?" the minister asked.

"No. But there are neighbors who I could stay with, until . . . until the new pastor is voted on and installed." She glanced up at the young man. "Perhaps my circumstances will be different in the spring."

"I have never found it wise to place too much hope on an outcome that is not guaranteed," the young man said.

She held herself with dignity as she stood, although Beau could see her lip trembling. She thanked the pastor, and he clutched her hands. They prayed for some moments and then he made a bow and walked into the back of the church. Miss McManus looked up at the young man.

"Is there no hope for us then, William?" she asked.

He tilted his head. "Surely you understand, Miss McManus. A minister must be upright in all his dealings. Especially in his choice of a wife."

"Nothing happened, William. There is no scandal for you to concern yourself with. I was kidnapped by a man who found me at my family's wagon," she said, and swallowed. "I was rescued by a person on his way to claim some property. He found me in the woods when I escaped and brought me back to Winchester."

"You wandered through the woods alone on that day, the day of your parents' death, until you made your way back here. Your nightdress was torn and you were hysterical. What do you think people thought of your appearance?"

Beau stared at the young man, most likely close to his age, in his black suit, all wrapped up in his own self-worth. The woman had been savagely treated and this man's concern was his own reputation. He'd best leave before he told the jackanapes what he thought of him. And then she began to cry.

"But William, don't you see? I have no one," she said as tears rolled down her face. "I have nowhere to go. We have corresponded for two years. We were to be married."

"None of this would have happened if you had obeyed me. I told you not to go back to your wagon. I told you! But you insisted! And what did it get you?"

"I had to go back. My parents were not buried. There were no words said over their graves. I begged you to go with me but you wouldn't. Why, William, why wouldn't you accompany me? You are right! None of the horribleness of the last six days would have happened if you would have gone with me!"

"We are not married! I could not ride out alone

with you! Young women should not be traipsing around the countryside with unmarried men, even if they are affianced. If you were not ruined on the day of your parents' death, your good reputation is gone now."

"William!" she whispered, and brought her hand to her lips, her eyes wide.

Beau had heard enough. He quickstepped to the man's blind side and punched him with all the anger that the woman must be feeling. The man reeled and Beau caught his shirt, stood him upright, and pummeled his midsection. He dropped to his knees in front of Beau and covered his head with his arms.

"You let a woman, your intended no less, ride out alone to bury her parents? You're a son-of-a-bitch!" Beau knelt down and grabbed the man's face in his hand and waited until their eyes met. "And you're going to hell. There's no doubt about that. You can wrap your sorry ass up in the vestments all you want. God will see you and remember you sending an innocent woman out into dangerous territory. You're going to hell for sure."

Beau stood, breathing hard, and looked back at Eleanor McManus. She was staring at him. "I'll take you to your wagon if you still want to go."

"Yes, Mr. Gentry. Thank you," she said in a

low, shaking voice. "I would appreciate that very much."

* * *

Eleanor settled herself in front of Mr. Gentry's furs on the mule with his help and all the dignity she could muster after wiping her eyes. How mortifying that he was witness to her humiliation! Where had he come from? Why had she gone back to William anyway? Had she expected a different answer? He'd already shunned her when he refused to help her bury her parents.

It occurred to her that nothing of her sheltered and planned life was proceeding as she'd anticipated or as her family had prepared her for. She could not imagine her mother or father ever encouraging her to remain in the company of a stranger, a man, with no ties to her family or church, but that was exactly what she was doing, perhaps because the only ones left who were acquainted with her family had left her to navigate on her own.

Mr. Gentry tied the horse and the mule to a post on the main street and helped her down. "We'll stop at the general store over there and pick up a shovel so I can dig your family's graves. I want to stop in here at the land agent first to check on my uncle's property."

Mr. Gentry guided her to the lone wooden chair in the office and turned, stepping to the counter to speak to two men poring over a massive map.

"What do you mean I need fifty dollars in silver to make my claim? I have the deed right here, and my uncle's will, and his death certificate," he said loudly after several minutes.

"Don't matter, son. You still have to pay the deed transfer, even with all the paperwork in order, which it looks to be."

"I don't have fifty dollars. I have forty. Will you take furs for the other ten?"

The older man shook his head. "Nope. You can sell your wares across the street. We take silver."

"And anyway, if you give us all your money, what are you going to do for a house or food? There's a cabin still there but it's been abandoned and probably ain't fit for living in. You going to stick your wife there in a lean-to 'til spring?" he said as he pointed at Eleanor.

Gentry picked up his papers, folded them neatly, and put them in a leather pouch. "There's no need for you to concern yourself with the comforts of those I'm responsible for. Good day to you, gentlemen. I will be back."

Eleanor rose, nodded at the men, and patted

Gentry's arm in consolation. He looked down at her hand and then into her eyes. What an intense man he was! She felt as if every inch of her were on fire, and she was certain she was blushing. She'd only meant to offer him comfort as his plans had gone awry as well as hers, but his forearm under her hand was muscled and thick and made her wonder who his wife would be. She would be a lucky woman to have this steadfast and determined man as a husband.

Gentry bought a shovel at the general store and tied it to his horse's saddle. They rode in the direction she gave him, and she felt sick and weak for what she might see. He was unsure as well, and offered several times to take her back to town while he did the burying. He would bring her back again to pray over their graves.

"No, Mr. Gentry," she said. "I will not be stripped of the chance to attend my family. I am the last of the McManus line if my aunt has gone on to heaven and will not shy away from unpleasantness. My mother and father never did. They deserve my ministrations."

"You do realize that varmints have already gotten to the bodies. They will not look like the people you remember. Maybe you should hang on to the pictures in your head rather than what I imagine will face us when we get there."

"My mother and father and sisters are no longer of this world. The Lord has them in his keeping and they feel no pain or sorrow. We are here in borrowed vessels, Mr. Gentry." She pointed. "There. There is the wagon."

It was as grim a scene as Beau suspected it would be. The flesh on the bodies was eaten by scavengers or rotting, he couldn't tell which, and there were only three bodies there, with tattered clothing and scraps around them. He suspected the missing one was in the woods somewhere, having been dragged off by a large animal or a pack of dogs. He dug four holes in some soft ground away from the road; it was hot work, even in the cool fall air. Eleanor stood for the longest time in the middle of the area where the bodies lay, silent, praying, he figured. She held a hand to her nose occasionally as the breeze carried the putrid smell of rotting flesh. She gathered rocks and made crosses with the stakes he'd taken from the back of the feed mill.

Beau took his rifle and followed a trail of broken grass into the woods. He didn't need to go far to find a woman's body with long hair. He laid down a piece of canvas he'd brought and pulled the body onto to it. He dragged it to the first hole and waited for Eleanor to turn to him. She came the short distance and he heard her sharp intake of breath.

"My mother," she whispered as tears tumbled down her face. "I can tell from her hair. My beautiful mother."

Eleanor dug through the valise she carried on the mule and covered the body with a dark green dress made of a shiny, fancy fabric. He waited 'til she stepped away and then began to shovel dirt onto the body. He helped her move the two smaller bodies, her sisters, she had said, Emily fifteen years old and Ruth just nine. She laid a homemade doll with the smallest of the two and a book of poetry with the larger one, before Beau covered them. It took them both to get her father onto the canvas and into the largest hole. He'd been a big man, Beau could tell, probably six feet or more, tall. Eleanor placed a crucifix, a bible, and a white collar on the man's chest before straightening. Finally, the bodies were covered with dirt and stones, with crosses pounded into the ground. She had written their names on each with a lead pencil she got from the wagon. He tied the shovel to his horse and waited.

"Mr. Gentry? Will you join me?"

Beau straightened his hair, tucked in his shirt, and walked over to the graves.

"Dear Lord, take the souls of my dearly departed family into your arms. Give them rest and comfort from whatever earthly torments they suffered," she began.

Eleanor McManus's voice was beautiful even when reciting a funeral dirge. He admired her, she who'd lost everything dear to her in a fragment of time and was still doing her part in the gruesome task that no young woman should have to do. He watched her make her pleas to the Almighty and could tell that she *believed*. Her God was real and beloved by her. He was jealous for a moment, nonsense he knew, as how could a flesh and blood man be jealous of the Lord. But he was.

"I will miss your quiet ways, Emily, and your kindness. Ruth, you were the light and laughter of this family. As our family's guiding light, Gordon McManus, Father, I will miss your steady hand and wise counsel."

Eleanor was silent for a long moment. Her voice hitched on her mother's name. "Olivia McManus. A most wonderful and gracious woman. I will aspire to be like you, to love as you did, to sacrifice as you did. I have been truly blessed by the Lord with a righteous, loving family."

She bowed her head, repeated the Lord's Prayer, and began to sing then in a clear beautiful voice that carried on the breeze and surely into the hills. He was mesmerized. There was no need for violins or harps or flutes to accompany her, every note rang clear.

"I shall profess, within the vale, a life of joy and peace."

Beau turned to his horse as she finished singing, adjusting the pack and the saddle, unable to steady his shaking hands. Had he ever been witness to such heartfelt love? He didn't think he had. She had loved them all with deep and profound feeling. He was humbled by her and unsure of himself suddenly. Nothing and no one had ever left him shaking or fearful or even in awe, until this very moment. She had changed him in some fundamental way that he did not yet understand. He turned when she called his name.

"You've done so much for me already, but I need your help," she said.

"What do you need? Where are you?"

"Under the buckboard."

Beau ducked under the wagon and found Eleanor picking at a piece of wood with a knife.

"I can't seem to budge it. Can you try?" she asked.

"What are we doing?" he said as he put his hand out for her to lay the knife in.

"There. Can you see the edge there? My father was brilliant, and I didn't believe him. Mother told me to believe in him, and yet I didn't!"

Beau raised his brows and looked at her face, now inches from his beneath the seat of the wagon. "Miss Eleanor. You're not making much sense."

"No. I'm not, am I? My father hid our silver money here. Those stupid, horrible thieves never even looked for it."

Beau turned back to where she pointed and examined the wood. It would have never been found unless someone knew where to look. But he hesitated to open it here, on a road where bandits lurked with nightfall not far, a young woman in his protection.

"I was thinking we should try and get the wagon back to town for you. It is yours, after all. You could sell it, and there are some boxes in the back that I imagine you will want to keep," he said.

"Yes. I was thinking the same thing but did not want to trouble you. They stole our horses, I imagine."

It was then he noticed four equine legs standing beside the wagon. "Nellie must have pulled loose where I tied her."

"No. That is not your horse," she said and scrambled out from under the wagon. "It is Bristol! She must have gotten away."

Beau watched her nuzzle the horse and heard

a neigh in return. "She doesn't look worse for the wear. Must have found some grasses to chew on."

Eleanor buried her face in the horse's mane. *Home, this horse and these belongings are what's left of home.* She would hang on to what remained of her past life, she must to maintain her sanity, but she would move forward in new directions. There was nothing gained by looking back, and her misery would never give life to her family again. She must honor them by remembering and living up to the ideals they held dear. She would look to the future and determine how she would continue on.

Mr. Gentry was watching her. "She will get the wagon to Winchester for us. We'll team her with Nellie and tie the mule to the back."

He took them directly to the stables and told the men working there that both horses and the mule should be brushed and fed, with an extra portion to the rescued horse. He moved the wagon to the area that the stable owner showed them.

"I've got a problem with that buckboard," Gentry said to the men. "I'd like to borrow a tool or two and fix it."

"We'll take care of it for you, mister," a young man said. "We worked on this one last week."

Gentry shook his head. "No. I prefer to do the work myself. If I could just borrow a chisel and hammer, I'd be much obliged."

The young man shrugged and pointed to a wooden box on the floor. "Hep yourself."

Eleanor waited as Mr. Gentry crawled under the wagon and came out a few moments later. He handed her a small, heavy metal box. She took it and put it in her valise that she found in the back of the wagon. It had been emptied, all her belongings dumped and rifled through, much of its contents on the floor of the wagon until she sorted her things and shook out her skirts and dresses.

"Is there a boardinghouse in this town?" he asked her as they left the stable.

"One that I know of. We stayed there while we were here in Winchester. The owner is a member of the church I visited." She looked up at him. "I'd prefer not to stay there."

"A hotel for you then? I will pay for your room," he said.

"I would appreciate that, as I would like to open this box in privacy, but I will pay you back as soon as it is open."

"There is no need for that."

"Yes, there is. You have a deed to be transferred and a dream to fulfill, Mr. Gentry. I will not burrow into your savings."

"I don't usually stay in a hotel. Too fancy and fine for the likes of me, but I do like to sleep in a real bed when I get the chance and I don't like the idea of you staying alone. I'll get a room near yours unless you think me presumptuous."

"I could hardly think you presumptuous. You've saved my life twice over."

She thanked him for his escort after he'd checked them in with the attendant in the lobby and paid for two rooms. She closed the hotel room door behind her and threw the bolt. She pulled the necklace that held her cross and a small key from around her neck, and inserted the key into the metal box. The mechanism turned soundlessly, and she lifted the lid. There were several gold coins and many more silver ones. She slowly opened a folded note.

Dear Wife or Daughter,

If you are reading this letter then you are in possession of the savings I've accumulated, much of which came from your mother's dowry when I married her before coming from England, as a minister's salary is not large nor is it regular. Whatever the circumstances are that you have opened this, remember to love the Lord and please him in all you do. I am ever so proud of all of you dear girls.

In Christ,
Father

Eleanor gave in then, alone and on her own, letting her falling tears turn into sobs. She would not dwell in this dark place for long but she was desperate for the release now. She cried until her eyes closed and she slept. She awoke later and knew that it would not do for her to continue on with sadness for even a short period of time, as she was on her own with decisions to make and without the luxury of idleness to consider her circumstances. She must determine how she would go on, what kind of employment she might secure, if she should attempt a trip by herself to Philadelphia to her aunt and pray that she was still in this world when she arrived, or if there was another path open to her. Unbidden, Mr. Gentry's face appeared before her eyes.

A note slid under her door.

Miss Eleanor. Eating at a restaurant near the hotel if you would care to join me.

Eleanor brushed out her hair, braided it, and pinned the braids around her head in a coronet. She put on her best outfit, a dark red plaid skirt with a white blouse and a short dark red jacket. She was happy to put on petticoats and clean drawers and stockings. She felt civilized and worthy of society. She felt like the young woman she was back in Allentown, ready to make the next step in her life, ready for her own story to unfold, past the danger and violence of the last week or more.

She opened the door after hearing a knock and Mr. Gentry's voice. He'd shaved his heavy beard and had his long hair cut. He was wearing a clean collarless shirt and a jacket. He looked handsome and masculine and a decade younger.

"Mr. Gentry," she said and smiled.

"Miss Eleanor."

Chapter Three

Beau realized at that moment Eleanor McManus was the woman he'd been dreaming of. All the solitary times, making his way from Canada, through foothills and over mountains, sometimes not seeing anyone for days, he'd dreamt of a woman. A woman who would comfort him and be his partner. A woman to love. Eleanor was that woman. The filmy image in his dream that woke him sweating with a roaring need to satisfy himself was real and alive and in front of him. She took his breath away.

"What shall I do with the box, Mr. Gentry?"

It was then he realized she was holding it in her hands. "I've put my deed and other documents in the hotel safe, but perhaps you would prefer I carried it for you."

"I would." She sat the box on the bed and turned, handing him a coin. "But first I want to pay you for this room."

"This is a twenty-dollar silver piece, Miss Eleanor. The room was only three-quarters of a dollar."

She stepped close and wrapped her hands around his and looked up into his eyes. "You must take it. How could I ever repay your bravery and kindness and steady companionship? Your toil over my family's graves? Your defense of me to a man not worthy to speak to you? You have been everything true, right, and gentlemanly. Please take it. You will be able to clear your uncle's deed."

Beau held her hands loosely and bowed his head. He was about to do the sort of thing that his mother scolded him for all those years ago. Speaking before thinking. Not considering consequences. But neither of those things were entirely true, if at all. He *had* considered the consequences as much as any man could. He'd thought about it for days if he was truthful with himself.

"There is something else you could do for me, Miss Eleanor. It is something far more precious, though, than a piece of silver," he said as he looked at her. She was staring up at him with wide green luminous eyes above rosy cheeks sprinkled with freckles, her hair in a shining crown. "Will you . . . will you marry me?"

She hesitated and licked her lips.

"I will do everything I can to see to your comfort. I will build you a home, and see that you are safe, warm, dry, and never hungry. I know it is quick and our meeting was less than ideal. I will give you as much time as you need to consider this. You have been through grave changes in a short period and I don't want you to be forced because you may feel obliged, even though there is no reason to."

"I corresponded with William for two years, and I knew nothing of his character, or the absence of it. Your character has been tested and tried from the day of our meeting. I will not change my mind. Yes, Mr. Gentry. I'd be honored to be your wife."

Beau inhaled sharply, feeling the elation of victory course through him, pounding in his ears and making his heart beat wildly in his chest. This was why men, the good ones, from centuries past and most likely in the distant future, too, laid down their lives for their womenfolk. His claim on her, and her willingness to accept him, felt like the triumph conquerors must have experienced when they laid waste to an army or stepped on a new land, as if they were kings of all they could see. He smiled crookedly at her.

"Are you ready for your meal, Miss Eleanor?"

Her face had gone bright red and she was blinking furiously. One tear trickled down her cheek. Beau's success wilted under the thought that a marriage to him would make this woman unhappy. He palmed her cheek and rubbed away her tear with his thumb.

"You needn't marry me, Miss Eleanor. I will see you situated somehow, somewhere safe and without worry, and be on my way. I will take you to Philadelphia to your aunt. Don't cry. I'll not impose on you any longer."

"No, no." She covered his hand with hers. "I am not crying because I am sad, Mr. Gentry."

She looked up at him then and dropped her eyes to his mouth. She licked her lips and leaned up to softly touch her lips to his cheek. He held completely still, perhaps from shock that this sheltered woman had kissed him or maybe that he didn't want the kiss to end. He could smell a lilac soap on her skin and see the gold flecks in her green eyes.

"Why are you crying then?" he whispered.

"Because my life has been turned upside down, and you have righted it. I have been dreaming that you might ask me this. I believe, even with all of the terrible things that have recently happened, I have been very blessed."

"My granny used to say some of the very best things in life are outcomes of the very worst things."

He escorted her to a restaurant a few doors away from the hotel, and Eleanor forced herself to stand tall, nod to others out on the street, and act with all the decorum and dignity her mother had taught her. In all likelihood, Winchester would be the town she would shop in, form friendships in, and attend church in, and she had no intention of allowing the townsfolk to shape an opinion about her that she did not deserve. She would soon be Mrs. Beauregard Gentry, and he, and the family they formed, would be respected in this town, if she had any say about it. The family they formed! *Oh dear!*

Even though she knew the general mechanics, her mother had promised her a more detailed and intimate description of the marriage bed before her and William's wedding. She had never thought that her mother would not be with her when she married, though. There were moments, many of them actually, when the last days seemed like a dream that she would awake from and her family would be with her and not cold in their graves. But it wasn't to be. She would never wake up and find a different outcome. Mother and Father and Emily and Ruth would still be dead if she lived to be one hundred years old. She looked up at Mr. Gentry.

"I am missing my parents. That is why I began to cry earlier. I wish you had known them and that they could have known you."

"You have much to be tender over, Miss Eleanor, but I do not wish to be one of the things that causes your grief."

"You are not. You are not at all."

They were seated across from each other in the busy room and ordered their food from a young woman.

"I would like to hear about your family in Louisiana, Mr. Gentry. You left home with an uncle, I believe you said."

"I am one of nine, although I am not sure where the hell my sisters and brothers are. My ma died when I was ten or so, and my pa was fond of his moonshine and didn't last much longer. Us kids were scattered to the wind when he died. Some went out to the Texas territories. I went to live with my Uncle Chester and Auntie Dorthea, although I'm not sure I was blood-related to either of them. I loved them, though, and they loved me. Aunt Dorthea was a teacher, and I am in her debt that I can read and cipher and know some histories."

"So you have no one?"

He shook his head. "Not after Uncle Chester died."

Eleanor reached across the table and touched his hand. "I'm very sorry."

"Tell me about your aunt in Philadelphia."

"There is little to say. I met her once when I was young, perhaps eight or nine years old. She is a spinster lady without family, and we lived far away from her. I remember hearing my mother say she was very angry when Father and Mother moved to Allentown shortly after I was born, to a new church. I believe they corresponded, but she was not known to me and Father never read her letters to us. I thought about going to her when I was unsure of my future, but Mother said her last letter was written by a neighbor because she was very ill. I wondered if I would get myself to Philadelphia and find that she had passed on. That won't be necessary now. I will have to write her and tell her of my upcoming marriage."

"I'm determined to make my mark, Miss Eleanor. You should know that. I won't be poor, or beholden to strangers, and I have done my adventuring. I want to claim my uncle's land. I want to pass on a stable, prosperous piece of property to sons and daughters," he said and looked at her steadily. "You may assure your aunt of that."

"I cannot think of a more satisfying plan than

the one you have just spoken of. Have you decided what you will do with your land? Will you farm?"

"Our land," he said. "When we're married, your name will be on the deed as well. I'm hoping that we'll be able to ride out soon and see for ourselves what this land is good for."

Her face had colored at the mention of sons and daughters, and the word *marriage*, invoked intimacies that were beyond her knowing. There were never conversations or discussions about procreation in her mother and father's household. She had never attended a birthing, which her mother did with some regularity. It was not done. Young Christian women in her church, her community, her *family* were chaste in thought and deed. How ridiculous, considering her present situation. There was nothing to guide her, other than her own instincts and the goodwill of her future husband. Perhaps that would be enough to lead her on the mysterious path of womanhood.

But one momentous thing had occurred. She was to be a landowner *with* him. She was to be a partner to him. She looked up at him and felt the strangest stirrings below her waist. His looks, the way fine hairs dusted his hands and peeked out from the top button of his shirt, the clean smell of him, and how his jacket lay tautly over broad shoulders appealed to her. And not just *appealed*.

That was far too tame a word. His lips and the way his dark eyes looked at her for a second longer than was polite had a pull beyond mere appearances. There was some magnetism between them she could not identify.

"It will be very exciting to see the land, our land, and begin to imagine what we can make of it," she said.

"It will be." He smiled at her.

Perhaps she was being foolish, or shortsighted, or wistful for the family roots she'd been accustomed to all of her life, she wasn't sure. But she was compelled, though, to say what she'd been thinking since very shortly after he'd asked her to marry him.

"I believe we should be married quite soon, if you're agreeable. Tomorrow or the next day."

She watched his Adam's apple bob and waited while he chewed and swallowed and took a drink of water. "I figured we'd want to take our time, seeing that you have relatives to mourn."

"No, Mr. Gentry. If we are to raise a family in this town, I intend to do so with no rumors or shadows cast on us. We cannot travel back and forth to our property, or spend all of our time together unless we are married. Our time at the cabin was an extraordinary circumstance, I believe, and you were the perfect gentleman. But now we are both safe from harm, and I have made a commitment to you, as it seems you have to me. In any case, two more weeks will not be enough to get to know each other in any significant way. If we are to be committed to each other, forge dreams and plans together, then I say we begin from the beginning."

"Miss Eleanor, won't you please call me Beau or Beauregard?" he said and took her hand. "I would have married you yesterday and all the yesterdays before that, if I'd known you then. But you are adrift. Perhaps when this is behind you a few more weeks, you will meet someone you'd rather marry or find something you would rather do altogether. I have said I will release you from your promise if so, and I meant it."

"I am as sure of this as I've ever been of anything in my life."

Beau did not see any misapprehension or doubt in her looks. In fact, he saw resolve, certainty, and practicality. "Then tomorrow it is."

She smiled at him then and applied herself to her meal. She took his breath away with her beauty and forthright nature. She would be everything he'd hoped to find in a wife, a partner.

As they walked back to the hotel, he stopped

them when there were no others around them and turned her to face him. "I do think it would be best if we waited until we had our cabin habitable before we... before we seal the marriage. I have no intentions of being together as man and wife on a small bed in a rented hotel room."

Her face bloomed red from her hairline to her chin. "Whatever you think is best, Mr. Gentry. Beau."

He would bet his last penny and all of Uncle Chester's property that Eleanor McManus was not only a virgin but also ignorant of the particulars. He sent a silent prayer aloft that he could make her first experience good enough that she'd want a second, a third, and an always.

"What do you mean you don't think you can marry us?" Beau asked the minister. He'd made his way back to the church that Eleanor had gone to when they first arrived in Winchester after he'd escorted her to her room and waited until he heard the lock on her door drop into place.

"Are you both quite sure this is what you want to do? After all Miss McManus has gone through, her parents' death and her own kidnapping? She may not be able to make a sound judgment in regards to something as permanent as marriage.

She may not even be in her right mind."

"Miss McManus is sane and is sure about her wishes. I have said the same things to her and she has not been moved."

Reverend Buckland offered him a seat in the first pew in the empty church and sat down beside him. "Young ladies can be so easily distracted from good sense by the events Miss McManus has experienced. And she may be still reeling from a broken heart," he said and stared at the altar.

"A broken heart? Over a man who would not help her give her family a Christian burial?" Beau shook his head. "Miss McManus has no veil over her eyes. She saw clearly what type of man her intended was."

"William was to be the assistant to Reverend McManus when they arrived in Charleston. It was only natural that the eldest daughter become his bride. She would have been planning this marriage from the time the reverend made his family aware of his plans for their new home and church. I'm still hoping that things can be resolved between them."

"She was fortunate to find out what a son-of-a-bitch her intended was before she became his wife."

Buckland turned sharply. "I cannot countenance that sort of language. We are in a house of worship! You are not the sort of man fit to marry a young woman from a good family such as Miss McManus. I feel an obligation to guide her in her father's absence, and I will do so!"

"But you were content to turn her away into the streets after her entire family was murdered," he said and rose. "There is no need for you to feel any obligation to Miss McManus. I will see to her welfare as you have not."

Beau walked out of the church as Buckland shouted at his back. He'd heard enough and made the long solitary walk to the hotel wondering what he would tell her.

"Miss Eleanor," he whispered as he rapped softly on her door. "I need to speak to you."

"What is it?" she asked as she opened the door a crack. "Is everything alright?"

"I just spoke to the minister at your church." He stopped as a pair of cowboys went past him in the hallway, and two women stepped onto the landing.

Eleanor pulled him inside and closed the door. She was wearing a white nightgown, embroidered and fussed up with ribbons at the collar, underneath a long blue robe that she'd tied at the waist with a sash. Her hair hung over her shoulder and down as low as her belly in a plait. Beau's mouth went dry.

"I shouldn't be in here," he said.

"We are to be married shortly, and I'd prefer not to discuss our private business in the hallway. What is it?"

"I visited with Reverend Buckland a few minutes ago."

"And what did the good reverend have to say?"

Beau twirled his hat in his hands. "I thought you'd like to be married in a church, so I went to talk to him this evening. He's . . . he's not inclined to marry us."

"Did he say why?"

"Well, in manner of speaking he did. He's concerned that you are still feeling the effects of recent events."

"I will tell him, if necessary, just as I've told you. I am not denying I'm feeling deep grief and loss over my family, and I was frightened beyond anything I could dream of when I was kidnapped. Young woman and men often marry quickly though, as life does not allow for lengthy engagements, and often marriages are arranged by parents, with little choice for either the bride or groom. But that is not the case for me. You are kind and steady in your defense of me and are planning to do great things with your life and the opportunities presented to you. Why *wouldn't* I wish to marry you?"

"Reverend Buckland thought you might be nursing a broken heart."

"I am. But it has nothing to do with William Dodgekins."

"So you will be satisfied going to the justice of the peace or the sheriff to be married?"

She looked up at him then, her eyes focused on his. "I wish to marry you. If I knew of another church in town, I would prefer that, but I don't, so we will be married by whoever can legally wed us."

"Then tomorrow it is." He leaned down to kiss her cheek, as she had done the day before, but she turned her head at the last moment, touching her lips to his. They both held still, barely meeting. He could feel the heat of her breath as it shortened and see her lashes lower. He pressed his lips to hers then and put a hand under her chin. "You are perfect," he whispered.

* * *

Eleanor held still, even though her heart was pounding in her chest. This was what she'd dreamt of as girl coming to womanhood. What she'd imagined in the dark of her bed, with the moonlight streaming in her room through the window back home after coming upon a couple in an embrace behind the schoolhouse one day. She'd stood there, near the lilac bush, intending to cut some blooms for the altar and smelling its heavenly fragrance, when she'd heard a low moan. At first she thought someone was hurt, but there wasn't pain in the sound. There was pleasure. She pulled a branch down and saw them. A young woman she knew and a handsome drifter who had been spending silver in the local saloon. His hat was tipped back and he held her arms and turned his head to cover the girl's mouth with his.

It was disturbing... and enticing. She'd run home that evening and raced through her chores and her lessons and gone to bed early, leaving her mother to think her head was aching. In bed, she curled on her side and closed her eyes to envision the man kissing the girl, to more closely examine where his hands were, where hers were, and what he was doing with his mouth. She wondered if her husband would kiss her like that, and when she met William, she dreamt about his embraces.

But this man, her husband to be, was kissing her and it felt nothing like what she'd imagined. There were no sweet songs playing off in the starry distance, no gauzy vision of a life ever after with happy smiles, and innocence. There was instead an eruption of emotion, of urges, of wants and needs, with no rational thoughts or even a girl's daydream to soften it. She was clinging to him, with her hands braced on his upper arms, where all that power resided. Where the strength to knock a man down with one punch and the steadiness to wield two deadly weapons was stored, yet his hand, his fingers on her chin and cheek, was exquisitely tender. She arched up on her toes to be closer.

Eleanor breathed in the scent of him. Of shaving soap, mint, and some faint note of male sweat, of masculinity, if there was such a thing. She let her fingertips travel up his arms to his shoulders, until she met with the bare skin of his neck and the tickle of his hair on her wrist. She held his head in her trembling hands, pushing her fingers through his hair and touching his ears with her thumbs. He moaned against her mouth; the feel of his breath against hers opened her lips to his. His hands circled her waist, holding her closer to him and letting the tips of her breasts sway against the hard planes of his chest, sending a shiver of nerves down her back and legs. *Ahhh!*

His tongue touched her bottom lip and trailed up to the corner, just grazing the inside of her mouth. Her eyes closed and she let herself feel all the sensations his touch caused without the bother or distraction of vision. He pulled away at that moment, breathing hard, and braced his forehead on hers.

"You will be my wife tomorrow," he whispered. "I can think of nothing but that and this."

She nodded. "And you will be my husband."

"I'm sorry you're disappointed about the church. The damned reverend made me mad. Maybe I could have convinced him if I hadn't lost my temper."

Eleanor looked up at him, determined to have her say, even if she was dim-witted and short-breathed from kissing him. "My father never used curse words."

Beau smiled. "Have I just been scolded by my bride to be?"

"Scolded?" She looked up at him. "Perhaps you do not want to take a bride who speaks her mind."

He held her face in his hands. "You would not be alive if you did not have a backbone, if you weren't courageous. I am in awe of you. Say what is on your mind, as I will. We will argue and disagree sometimes, but isn't that the nature of marriage?"

"My mother and father did not argue often, and when they did it was always behind closed doors. But they kissed each other's cheeks and held hands and hugged and told each they loved each other in front of us. I never doubted, even on the rare occasion when I did hear angry voices, that they were truly in love and respected each other."

"A fine example for us to live up to."

Chapter Four

"I have had a lovely day, husband," Eleanor said at the door of her room the following evening. "Our meal at the hotel dining room was very grand, and I'll remember it forever."

"We've got our deed and our wedding license, signed and sealed," he said, and patted his breast pocket.

"Will we visit the property tomorrow?"

"I would like to, Eleanor." He smiled at her and held her hands in his.

"I want to thank you, Beauregard," she said softly. "I am honored to be your wife and will do my best to make a home, and raise children you will be proud of. I cannot tell you how much it meant to me that you escorted me to church and waited while I said my prayers and spoke to Reverend Buckland."

He shook his head. "You don't have to thank me for such small matters. You are my wife. If you need escorted, I hold that privilege."

"You remind me so very much of my father. He was always so kind to Mother. And thank you for taking me to their graves today. It may have seemed morbid for a wedding day but for . . ."

Beau wrapped her in his arms as she began to sob. "They are still very alive to you. It is only a short time ago that you spoke to them and touched them."

She nodded against his chest. "I felt as if I had to tell them, especially my father, that I was married and that you were a good man and that he could be sure that I would be taken care of and protected. It sounds very silly as I say it."

"It is not silly. It is not silly at all." He leaned her back in the circle of his arms. "I'm no religious man. I just don't take to it and don't know that I ever will. But I made my peace with your daddy, too, today. He deserved to hear my promises to keep you safe."

Eleanor opened the door to her room. "I look forward to tomorrow, Beauregard."

He kissed her forehead and waited in the hall until she locked the door to her room. She undressed in the dim light of the kerosene lamp then curled under the covers and shivered. Soon, she thought, she wouldn't shiver in the night from the cold sheets and damp air. Soon she would climb in bed with Beauregard. Her husband. How happy she was! How strange life could be. Emptiness and fear and desolation could be overcome by joy and bittersweet memories . . . and longing. She was hungry for him, she admitted to herself, and worried she was no longer in control of her nineteen-year-old body. How could it be a "duty," as her mother reluctantly described, if she wanted it, whatever "it" was, so badly. Although her mother had smiled when she said it and told her that joining with her husband was so much more than that, so much more than a duty, and that she would tell her about the mysteries in good time.

There would be no good time now. How strange to wish to feel a man she did not know, had not heard of, less than a month ago. She wished she could run her hands over his shoulders and touch the hair on his chest. She wanted to feel his hand touching her, touching her everywhere, especially her breasts, heavy now with the thought of him undressing. Would he touch her there? In her most private, intimate area that she had no name for? He would have to, she imagined, if what she thought was necessary to complete the act happened. Would his hand touch her there with feather traces like when he stroked her cheek with his long fingers? The bed was suddenly cozy and warm as she replayed their kisses in her head, and she fell asleep as she twirled the gold wedding band on her finger.

* * *

Beau knocked on his wife's door, *his wife!*, he thought in some wonder, and waited.

"Good morning, Beauregard," Eleanor said, smiling and rosy cheeked, when she opened her door.

"Good morning. I want to have the men at the stable check the wheels on the wagon. I thought we'd take it out this morning to find our property. It may take some time at the stables. Would you like to wait here?"

She pulled on a straw poke bonnet and tied the wide blue ribbon under one ear. "I'll go to the mercantile while you are at the stable. You can bring the wagon there when you're done, if that is agreeable to you."

"By yourself?" he said and twirled his hat in his hand.

She turned to him. "I imagine I will be by myself as you'll be at the stables. We did not bring many of the things I'll need in a household from Allentown, as my mother intended to purchase items when we arrived. I don't mean to purchase much, but I'll need soap and salt, at the very least. Could you see if there are any burlap sacks to be had at the mill?"

"Could you wait until I'm finished at the stable?"

Eleanor tilted her head and stared at him. "I went to the mercantile by myself when we stayed here. Reverend Buckland told my father it was perfectly fine for me to go alone during the day. I went several times and took my sisters on some occasions, too."

Beau had seen women of all ages walking alone out in the town over the last few days, but they had not been his wife. She was staring at him now with raised brows. "Just be careful. There are always drifters coming though towns like this."

She smiled up at him, and he realized he would most likely grant her anything to see her smile and her eyes crinkle up at the corners. He escorted her down the street with a hand under her elbow, past horses, buggies, and troughs 'til she was at the door of the mercantile.

"Be about an hour, I think, and I'll come by for you."

"Thank you. That will be fine," she said as she

pulled a paper from her bag and whisked herself past pickle barrels and into the store.

* * *

"Which fabric would you recommend for making a tick for my bed, or do you sell ready-made ones?" Eleanor asked the woman behind the counter as she ran a hand over the canvas. She looked up when the woman didn't answer.

"Aren't you the daughter of that preacher who got himself killed?"

"My father and mother and sisters were murdered by outlaws, just outside of your town, yes."

"Not that it's any of my business, but what do you need a tick for?"

"I was married yesterday. I'll be setting up housekeeping soon."

The woman's eyes widened. "William took you back?"

Eleanor kept her face expressionless as she realized other shoppers had inched closer to hear her reply. "I have not married Mr. Dodgekins, if that is to whom you refer. *Do* you carry ready-made ticks?"

She refused to be drawn into this conversation, and realized that her family's story, and its outcome, was most likely repeated at every opportunity. She would muster all the dignity necessary to quell such talk. And then the door of the mercantile opened behind her.

"Eleanor, my dear!"

She turned in time to be pulled into Reverend Buckland's wife's arms and patted on the back as if she were a small child.

"I am so terribly sorry I was not here in your time of need, Eleanor. I've been attending my niece who has just presented her husband with a son. What a horrible event for your family! I am so sorry for you! Please come back with me to the church. We will discuss your future, and you may unburden yourself of whatever upsetting memories you have."

Eleanor pulled herself out of the woman's arms. "Mrs. Buckland, thank you very kindly for your sympathies. I have set a course for myself, however, and my future is well planned."

"Well planned? I heard that our William was less than sympathetic when he heard about the event, poor man, and undoubtedly said some things that he shouldn't have. But he is heartbroken now. You must come back with me to the rectory. I will make tea and we will see how to make this right. It is only what your poor sainted mother would have expected."

"Not today, Mrs. Buckland. I will call on you soon, though."

"Said she was already married, Mariam," the woman behind the counter said.

"Already married? Whatever do you mean?"

Mrs. Buckland's grip on her upper arms tightened, and Eleanor forced herself to stand straight and not be intimidated. What hold did this woman have over her, anyway?

"I am married, Mrs. Buckland. Yesterday, to be precise. I am now Mrs. Beauregard Gentry. He has been willed property in this county and we—"

"Not that man!" she shouted. "Not that man who hit William!"

"Mrs. Buckland, please, calm yourself," Eleanor said and looked around at the others in the store, all now in a hurry to look away. "There is no need for shouting."

Miriam Buckland dabbed at her eyes and shook her head. "With your mother gone and myself away, you've been set adrift alone. The reverend and I were talking shortly after that night that we would take you in to our home. Yet with me being out of town, I had no idea what had happened. Something must be done!"

"There is nothing to be done. I am married and glad of it."

The older woman grabbed her hands and

squeezed. "Please come with me to the rectory. Please allow me to talk to you. I feel so terribly guilty having not been here in your time of need. And certainly, between the reverend and I we can solve this problem."

"There is no problem," Eleanor began, and realized at that moment that she must end this once and for all if she were not to have this story follow her into eternity. She nodded. "Let us go to the rectory. I will be happy to take tea with you and explain what has happened."

She stopped and turned to the woman behind the counter. "My husband, Mr. Beauregard Gentry, will be here for me shortly. Please tell him to wait and that I will be back very soon."

* * *

Beau made good use of his time while the blacksmith fixed a spring on the McManus wagon. He followed the stable master, asking questions and being friendly and helpful. Very soon, he was being introduced to every man who came in the stables, shaking their hands and listening as they talked. Whenever he could, he asked the men what they made their living at. Some farmed corn and sold it as silage to the dairy farmers or shipped it to be ground. The dairy farmers made cheese, some of it going as far away as Philadelphia. Most farmers grew wheat, ground at the gristmill and bagged to send by train or wagon to cities. What he didn't hear was that anyone was breeding and selling horses to pull their wagons and plows or to ride. He could hardly wait to tell Eleanor.

He pulled up to the mercantile in the wagon nearly two hours after he'd dropped her off. He didn't see her standing outside the building, so he pulled the wagon over and hitched the horses to the post. He looked in the window of the store and finally pulled the door and went in.

"There's a young lady doing her shopping here," he said to the woman behind the counter, "Miss McManus you'd know her as. Is she here? I'm a mite late."

"I don't know who you're talking about," the woman said.

"I let her off here a couple of hours ago. She meant to buy some salt and whatnot. She must be here somewhere."

A man behind the counter came over to stand beside the woman. "She went with the reverend's wife. Mrs. Buckland."

"Shush, Henry. It's none of our business," the woman said, but would not meet Beau's eye.

Beau nodded to the man, too angry to even look at the woman. "Much obliged."

***

Eleanor sat on the edge of the brocade chair, her back straight, her face and hands as calm as she could manage. "Thank you," she said and accepted tea from Mrs. Buckland. She'd been alone in the sitting room for nearly a quarter of an hour, waiting for her hostess and wondering what had become of the woman.

"Now, dear," Mrs. Buckland said, reached over, and patted her hand. "We are private without the gentlemen. Tell me what happened, Eleanor."

She recounted the night of her parents' deaths, without revealing her mother's humiliation, as she had no intention of this woman having any vision of her mother and her family that was not completely proper and upright, even knowing her mother had done nothing but try and shield her children. But the reverend's wife was of the temperament her father abhorred, and she knew full well that the woman would share everything that was said between them. Eleanor intended to guard her family's dignity.

"And then I went to our wagon to bury my family and was kidnapped."

Mrs. Buckland titled her head. "Why did you go alone, dear? What could you have been thinking?"

"I had no one to ask after Mr. Dodgekins refused to help me, ma'am, and my family needed a proper burial."

"I'm sure William would have gone with you eventually. He was very upset about the entire event, as I'm sure you know. Sometimes we just need to be patient with our men while they sort out the best path forward for themselves and their womenfolk."

"I don't believe that is true," Eleanor said and sat her china teacup on the cart. "And I had no intention of letting animals prey on their bodies, although that is what happened anyway."

"William did say you came here after you'd been freed from your kidnapper but that he was startled at the sight of you. He did believe you'd been killed and was mourning you deeply, you understand that he was in shock, rightfully so, and perhaps did not answer your questions well. And then that barbarian hit him! A man of God!"

There was so many falsehoods in what was just said, Eleanor was at a loss as to how to correct the woman, but she couldn't be silent. Her father had preached many a sermon whose lesson was to honor and defend the truth and righteousness, even when it was easier and advantageous to be silent.

"No, Mrs. Buckland. That is not what happened

at all. I was there, you see. Mr. Dodgekins was not mourning me; he was disgusted by me and told me so to my face."

The woman shook her head vigorously. "No, no. I am certain you have misinterpreted what was said. How did you eventually get free?"

"I was moments away from being sold to bandits when Mr. Gentry saved me. He killed the men and my kidnapper. He took me to a cabin and let me rest and heal until I was well enough to travel. I don't remember all of it, as it had been several days that I had gone without food and had hit my head somewhere along the way, I'm not sure where. And then he brought me to Winchester, and I came here immediately." Eleanor looked up at the woman and held her gaze. "I expected to be welcomed by the church family I'd met here and by Mr. Dodgekins, who was, to my understanding, intending to marry me and assist my father when we arrived in Charleston."

"William, I am certain, will be asked to travel to Charleston and lead the congregation there since your father's unfortunate demise. He will need a wife, Eleanor. A sensible wife who understands the church and the exalted place her husband holds in it. Even with this minor setback, you are the perfect wife for him."

"I would not characterize my family's murder

as a minor setback, and it is an impossibility anyway, as I'm already married to Mr. Gentry."

Mrs. Buckland moved her chair close to Eleanor until their knees nearly touched and held both her hands. She leaned forward and then began to speak in a soft voice near Eleanor's ear.

"There is a way forward on God's path for you." She paused. "Did you lay with this man while you were in the woods?"

Eleanor felt herself redden. "Of course not," she said quietly. "I was injured, and he was a perfect gentleman."

Mrs. Buckland backed up just an inch or so to see Eleanor's face. "And have you lain with him since?"

Eleanor shook her head and immediately knew her mistake, although was it ever a mistake to tell the truth? "No, ma'am. We are preparing our home on his property, even today. I must go, in fact. Mr. Gentry will be concerned about me."

"Let us pray over this. Dear Father . . ."

Eleanor closed her eyes and willed herself to be humble and contrite in prayer, even though she was horribly angry. Shortly after they loudly said "amen," Reverend Buckland and Mr. Dodgekins came into the parlor.

"Ah, my dear," the reverend said and took both of her hands in his while his wife moved her chair back. "How well you look today. And see who is here to make his greeting to you."

Dodgekins pulled a chair close to hers and reached for her hand. Eleanor looked at him sharply and laced her fingers together. "It would be improper for me to hold your hand, sir, and please move your chair away from mine. I am married."

"To that brute? Certainly you realize that he is not suited to you. I am a man of God as you are accustomed to, just like your dear father who has gone on to his reward."

"I was not suited to *you* when I came asking for your help, was I?"

"I was out of my mind with worry, Eleanor, and not thinking clearly."

"Mrs. Gentry, if you please."

Reverend Buckland cleared his throat and then spoke up from beside his wife. "An annulment will not be difficult. You were not married in the church, and there were extraordinary circumstances surrounding the events that may have lead you to make an undesirable decision. And, well, the marriage, I understand, has not been . . . made sacrosanct."

"That beast," Dodgekins said scornfully. "It pains me to think of him and you, the most delicate and pious of women."

"I must be going now, Mrs. Buckland. Thank you so much for the tea," Eleanor said as she rose.

"Life will be ever so difficult without friends to help you," the woman said, staring up at Eleanor with pursed lips.

"We feel obligated to ensure your well-being with your dear father cold in the grave. There are papers for you to sign in my office that will put the matter behind you," Reverend Buckland said.

"There is no matter to put behind me. I am married to Mr. Gentry and have no wish to annul it."

Dodgekins stared out the window, legs crossed, his hand at his chin. "It is difficult to lead a faithful life to the Lord. We must admit our mistakes and allow those with experience and wisdom to lead us to what is good and right in His eyes." He looked up at her then. "Isn't that what your father said when he spoke to the congregation here that fateful Sunday?"

Eleanor choked back a sob and dropped into the chair behind her. *Father!*

They all turned when there was a knock on the main door of the house, followed moments later by pounding. The reverend opened the door to the sitting room, and Eleanor saw an elderly woman hurry by in the hallway.

"Eleanor!" she heard from outside.

She stood quickly. "Beau! I am here. I am coming." She maneuvered her way through the chairs, past the tea cart, and pardoned herself to the reverend, who was blocking the doorway.

The elderly woman opened the front door, and Eleanor rushed by her.

"I am so very glad to see you," she said and led him down the rectory's stone path.

Beau followed his wife, matching her hurried pace. She slowed down finally. and he cupped her elbow. "Your face is pure white. They have upset you. I swear I will never set foot in that place again or even speak to those vermin."

"Please take me somewhere private where we can talk without interruption."

"We'll go back to your room."

Eleanor sat down on her bed in her hotel room and removed her hat. Beau leaned against the wardrobe near the door. She looked up at him, still white-faced, and licked her lips.

"I went with Mrs. Buckland because she was making a scene in the mercantile. I wanted to quiet her and felt in some way that I owed her an explanation or at least the whole story as my family had been guests in their home many times for meals and fetes. Father had preached from their altar."

"And?" he said when she said no more.

"Mrs. Buckland said that William Dodgekins was shocked only, accounting for his blunt words on both occasions that I asked for his help, and that I needed to be patient with him until he decided our future. Mr. Dodgekins himself told me he was quite out of his mind with worry for me."

There was little Beau could do to tamp down the anger he was feeling. It was coming from an unknown place, perhaps his heart, he thought suddenly. He felt the blood rising on his face, and sweat bead on his forehead, although it was not hot in the room. His arms hung loose at his side, as if anticipating an attack. He cracked his neck from side to side.

"What else?"

"Mr. Dodgekins reminded me of part of my father's sermon when he spoke about leading a faithful life and bowing to the wisdom of elders after one has made a mistake. It was the last sermon he preached. The words were dear to me, and I believe that Mr. Dodgekins realized that. I could hear father's voice in my head and feel my mother's hand as if . . ."

Beau heard Eleanor's plaintive words over

the red, hot fury that he was feeling and forced himself to take a few breaths. But it was alive in him, this rage that was making him want to kill William Dodgekins, strangle him, and watch the bastard's eyes pop out and eventually roll back in his head.

"Have you made a mistake, Eleanor? Would your father want something different for you?"

"No. I have not made a mistake. I have not. You have done nothing but honor me and protect me since I have met you. Father would be pleased, I am sure."

There was a long silence that Beau hesitated to break. "But are you pleased?"

She stood then and faced him. "I am happy with my choice. Very happy. Even still, I would honor our commitment regardless. We are married."

She turned away quickly and busied herself with her hat and bag and smoothed the spread on the bed where there was not a wrinkle to be seen.

"What else did they say, Eleanor? There is something you are not telling me."

She worried the strings on her cloth purse and spoke softly. "She asked me . . . she asked me if we'd lain together, and I said no. Reverend Buckland said the marriage had not been made complete in the eyes of the church then. He had papers in his office for me to sign to annul our marriage."

"Is that what you want?"

"No. No." She looked up at him. "I do not want an annulment. I would have never signed anything. It was just difficult with all of them talking. It felt like what I was used to hearing—church folks talking. I wanted to leave, I'd even stood to leave, and then William quoted my father's last sermon and it was clear to me then that I have chosen a life divorced from all I've ever known. It was an uncomfortable moment. But still just a moment."

Beau knew his wife was talking. Knew rationally that she was explaining something to him, but he could not hear any of it. He could only hear "annulment" and "had not been made complete" reverberating in his head. She was not yet his woman in their eyes, their union not solidified enough, and his anger suddenly had a new direction. A raw, unchecked passion. He would not give her up. She was his for time immortal, and he would make his mark on her and put to rest any thoughts from any other man that she would be anyone's but his.

Beau pulled her into his arms and kissed her roughly, pulling pins from her hair as he did and twisting his hand in the loosened strands to hold her head still and allow him to kiss her at his pleasure. He felt her hands around his waist circling up to his arms, lightly touching his shoulders. He ran a hand up her side, cupping her breast and rubbing the hard peak through the starched pleats of her blouse. She moaned in his mouth and he swung her down until she lay across the bed, her chest heaving as she drew each breath through an open mouth, her eyelids drooping. With one knee on the bed, he pulled her skirts to her waist and ran a hand between her legs 'til he found the opening in her drawers. She was wet already and hot to the touch, groaning with each stroke. He pulled his belt from his pants and opened the button fly. With his cock in one hand, he watched her moving on the bed and gripping the coverlet while his fingers stroked her. He meant to bury himself in her deep and hard.

"Beau," she said softly.

And that one word from her stopped him cold. It was his Eleanor he was doing this to. His wife. Surely virginal as much as the stars were in the sky, and here he was going after her as if she were a two-penny whore.

He pulled her skirts down and his shirt out to cover his erection and lay down beside her, one arm across his face. "Oh God, Eleanor. I am so sorry. I am treating you roughly, something I swore I would never do."

"It is alright. You are my husband," she said breathlessly.

"When you said they wanted you to get an annulment because we had not had relations, I went a little crazy," he said with a half laugh. "But you are not a mare that I will brand. You are my wife and deserve tenderness and care."

She rolled up on her side against him. She put her lips on his and touched her tongue to his bottom lip. "I don't know what to do, husband, other than what you have already shown me. But I want more. I want all of it," she said. "Reveal the mystery to me."

Eleanor had never had anything feel the way it did when Beau touched her with his fingers. It seemed as though her entire lower insides were going to explode, as if his fingers were a match to tinder. She had watched his face and the change in him from furious anger to a passion for her that ignited her need for him. He was going to make sure there was never a possibility of an annulment. They would be truly man and wife, and she craved it. He held her in an embrace she would not be able to break physically, yet one word from her had stopped him. But she wanted his passion, she wanted his hands on her bare breasts, holding her head still with a fistful of her hair. She wanted his hand lower. Even thinking about it made her legs shift restlessly against him.

"Show me," she whispered against his ear.

Beau rolled and loomed over her. He unbuttoned her blouse with shaking fingers, glancing at her and finally pulling her chemise down until her breasts were bare. Breathing hard, he licked his lips and leaned down, sucking her nipple into his mouth. She called out and arched off the mattress as his hand went back under her skirts. Within moments, her legs were open to him, and she pushed off of his fingers as he moved them inside of her and out. There was a tempest building in her, swirling her up in its path, quickening in rhythm and intensity, her hands digging in his hair as if it would hold her grounded.

He climbed on top of her. She looked between their bodies to where he was guiding himself, into where his fingers had been. He slid in slowly, stretching her as he went until he breached her virginity, finally taking the last bit with a lunge that arched her back. He moved in and out of her, and she felt the storm rise again. She met him thrust for thrust, hearing some wet sound and tasting his mouth as he found hers again in an urgent kiss that matched the movement of his hips. *This* was the mystery. This joining of him and her to be one, she thought as she exploded and cried out. Then he stilled above her with one violent thrust and a last shudder, dropping his head to her breast and kissing her neck and ear.

He rolled off of her then, sweating and panting, red-faced and still breathing hard. He ran a hand under her neck and pulled her toward him until she was tucked against his side, her head on his shoulder, reveling in the heat and the smell of him.

"It is daylight, Beau," she whispered. "We have not yet eaten our noonday meal."

His shoulder shook under her head as he barked a laugh. "There is no right or wrong time to do this, Eleanor. We can make love in the light of day and in the still of the night. And I intend to do just that."

"Is that what this is? Making love?"

He tilted her head up with his hand and kissed her open-mouthed, and spoke even as their lips still touched. "I don't know of any other way to describe it—not the act or how I feel about you—as anything but love. I never imagined myself loving anything or anyone. But I will love you until the last moment of my life and beyond into the evermore. I am sure of it."

She stared back at him. "My mother told me that most times love comes slowly to a married couple. I cannot see that. I could not have done what I have just done with you without my heart engaged. Without love."

"We are well and truly married."

"We are," she said and sighed contentedly.

"Perhaps I will stop to see the reverend and his wife and let them know."

She propped herself on an elbow. "Beauregard! You wouldn't dare! I would be mortified!"

He rubbed her back. "I would never embarrass you, Eleanor. I was teasing you. But that does not stop me from imagining the looks on their faces when I announced that I'd been under your skirts!"

Eleanor felt her face redden and laughed. "It would be a sight!"

"Shall we go and see our property?" he asked.

"Yes. Let me straighten my hair and rinse my face," she said as she sat up. She looked back at him, still stretched out on her bed, looking manly and satisfied with his life. What a marvel, she thought to herself, to be married to a man she could laugh with, who made her feel wanted and precious, who protected her with his hands and his heart. Who did *that* to her body.

"We could have a child growing in you right this moment, Eleanor," he whispered. "Did you realize that?"

She nodded. "I will pray it is so."

Chapter Five

Beau and Eleanor rode in the wagon together on a two-wheel path near the edge of a deep forest and he repeated all he had learned at the stables that morning. Eleanor agreed that raising horses might be just the thing for them. Beau consulted the map the surveyor had given him and the hand-drawn directions given to him by the dairy farmer. The sun was shining but the air was cold and dry, and Beau found a blanket in the back of the wagon to put over Eleanor's legs. He spotted the outcropping of rocks to the north just as the dairy farmer had told him he would. Beau turned the wagon to pass the rocks and pulled the horses to a stop as a valley came into view. He pointed with his free hand to a cabin situated on the opposite side of the valley on a plateau of flat land.

He checked his pocket watch and saw that they were only three-quarters of an hour from town, even though there was not a sign of civilization as far as he could see. Not another cabin, or a fence, or even billow of smoke from a fireplace as he surveyed the horizon and guided the wagon up a gentle slope. Neither he nor Eleanor spoke a word as they rode to the cabin. The valley, even with the stark gray of the naked trees and browned grasses, was a beautiful sight, and he knew she agreed, as she gripped his hand where he held the reins and looked out over the vista before them.

"It is a paradise," she whispered as they came to the flat land where the cabin sat.

"Maybe that's what we'll call it. Paradise."

He helped her down from the wagon, and she followed him to the door. When it didn't move easily, he put his shoulder to it and opened it with a creak of dry wood. He heard a match strike behind him, and the soft glow of a candle Eleanor held lit the shadows. It was a large one-room structure with a massive stone fireplace against one end. There was a table and a chair near a sink with a pump handle. He walked to it and tried to move the handle, but it was rusted in place.

"One of the men at the stables I met, a dairy farmer who lives west of us, told me he knew the old man who lived here and had visited a few times. He said the well was a good steady one with clean water and that we'd find a small stream for livestock behind the house near the trees."

"There is a bed frame here," Eleanor said. "It seems sturdy enough. I need to get ticking to make us a mattress. There are sheets and blankets in the wagon in a trunk. We will need lamps."

"What do you think, Eleanor?"

She turned to look at him. "I think this is where we will raise our children, where we will raise horses to make our living, where our dreams will come true."

He pulled the door shut and pointed to just above where the valley began to slope inward. "I'll build our stables there, where we can easily have grain delivered, and a corral for good weather. We will look in the barn tomorrow. The days are getting shorter and I don't want to be caught on this path after dark until I know it better."

Eleanor was busy with her pencil and paper. "I will need to make purchases at the mercantile."

"I have several good pelts I have not sold yet in the saddlebags. We will get as much as we can for them and use the money to get us through the winter. We must be careful with your silver. It's got to buy us our studs and get us through one more season until we are able to begin selling foals."

"I will put in a kitchen garden, and I know how to can and dry meats."

Beau helped her settle on the seat of the wagon. "I imagine there are plenty of deer in the woods. I will get a henhouse together for the spring."

He climbed onto to the buckboard, clicked the horses in motion, and looked at Eleanor as she concentrated on her list on the paper on her lap. The wind began to blow and the temperature dropped rapidly, and he focused on keeping Bristol on the path. When he looked at Eleanor again she was gazing into the wooded landscape and her lip was trembling.

He helped her down from the wagon at the stables and followed her to the restaurant where they had eaten many of their meals.

"Is something bothering you, Eleanor?" he asked after the cook had brought them bowls of stew and slices of crusty bread.

"No," she said and moved the potatoes around in her bowl. She looked up. "I hate to bring it up as we've had such a wonderful day, even aside from Mrs. Buckland. Our home is beautiful. I am so very fortunate to have it, to be married to you with all of our lives before us and so much to look forward to. But it is December. My mother would have been planning her baking and making or buying gifts for us girls. We would be getting ready for the church service to celebrate the birth of Christ. It was always my very favorite time of year. This year will be very solemn and quiet."

"I will take you to church, but I won't go inside. I don't want anything to do with Buckland," Beau said and looked up at her. "And honestly, I wish you wouldn't go either. They have done nothing but treat you poorly. They don't deserve your kindness."

"I will not allow them to come between myself and the Lord. I miss my family desperately all of the time, but Christmas will be especially hard."

Eleanor sat quietly through the rest of the meal, watching her husband wipe his bowl clean with a heel of bread. She was lucky in so many ways, and she would focus her thoughts on those things and keep at bay the overwhelming sense of loss that crept into her mind. It happened at the strangest times and when she was least prepared for the heart pounding and dry throat that accompanied a sudden vision. Riding back to town in the wagon, she'd been excited to make her list of things she would need to make the cabin a home, and then she looked off in the distance trying to decide how many oil lamps she should purchase and saw a straggly pine standing alone away from the forest of bare trees and evergreens. There was a moment, just a fleeting moment, where she saw her sister's smiling face, so real that she lifted a hand to touch Ruth's cheek.

"Eleanor?"

"Oh," she said. "I am so sorry. I was lost in a daydream. What did you say?"

"I asked what kinds of things your family did at Christmastime." He was leaning forward, across the table from her, attentive, his hands wrapped around a metal mug of coffee.

"There are so many good memories," she said with a wistful smile. "So many. Mother making the shortbread dough, rolling it out, and letting us cut shapes before she sprinkled them with sugar and baked them. Getting new hair ribbons or lace collars or sacks with clear candy or chocolate on Christmas morning. Walking into the church on Christmas Day and seeing the fruit of my mother's and some other church women's labors: The pews and altar would be draped with boughs of fresh pine and ribbons. It was beautiful. On Christmas Eve we sang carols while my mother played the piano, and afterwards we would visit the poorest family in our town and take them socks she had knitted and food she'd made or collected.

"A German family belonged to our church, and Father liked their tradition of cutting down a pine tree for in the house. We would hang paper ornaments on it, and Mother would scold him for finding the most ill-shaped and crooked tree in the woods. Most of all I can hear my father preach about the wonder of the Savior's birth. There was not another sound in the church other than his voice as he read the story."

Beau reached for her hand. "You are very lucky to have those memories."

"I am. Was there anything special about Christmas for you when you were younger?"

"We didn't go to church too much; Aunt Dorthea did more regularly. Uncle Chester was convinced the traveling preacher was stealing from the collection plate," he said with a chuckle. "I don't think he was, but Chester didn't take well to the man and he rarely went, so I didn't either. We always went to dinner at some relative of Aunt Dorthea's on Christmas Day, and I had to clean good under my nails and wear new stiff clothes and slick my hair down. It was a trial."

"I can imagine you were a bit of a trial to your aunt and uncle." She smiled.

"I was. But they loved me, and I loved them back. So I guess that made all the difference."

"It does," she whispered and then straightened in her seat. "I refuse to be maudlin. I will miss them every day, but I won't be sad on their account. None of them would have wanted me to. They would have wished me to be joyful, just as I would if it had been one of them to live. I would want them to remember me and be happy."

* * *

It was December twenty-third, and Beau had bought a used cookstove and hauled it to the cabin just a few days prior with the help of two men he'd met at the stables. Eleanor had scrubbed it and loaded it with logs and was hoping that she could produce some shortbread like her mother had always done. She turned the pages of her mother's recipe book, reading the handwritten notes and remembering the time she'd spent with her in their Allentown home, the smell of cinnamon and cloves in the toasty kitchen, her mother's white apron with bits of sugar and flour where she she'd wiped her fingers, and the welcome gust of cold air when her father opened the door carrying whatever supply her mother had sent him looking for.

Two weeks' worth of daytime had flown by as they had worked in the cabin and on their property to prepare for a winter that was already upon them. Eleanor had continued to stay at the hotel at night while Beau stayed in the cabin, guarding their homestead. They had finally unloaded the end of the boxes and trunks from her family's wagon, and she'd spread out the bedding her mother had packed along with a quilt hand-sewn by the members of their church as a parting gift to their family.

She bought flour, sugar, lard, and salt for the larder near the sink and bacon, a few apples left from the fall harvest, and cream in a metal tin that she was thinking she'd have to store outside, up and away from animals but cold enough to keep them. She'd just put a tablecloth and one of the new lamps she purchased on the small table they would eat at when the door opened.

"I'm muddy, Eleanor. Come hand me the cream and bacon and give me a kiss. I've found a springhouse," Beau said.

"A springhouse?"

"It's not far from the cabin. The steps are rotted but the door is solid, and there are even shelves in the stone and hooks to hang a ham or buckets of milk."

She handed him the bacon. "I'm going to use the cream and bake us some shortbread for Christmas. What is that?" she asked when she looked down at the ground.

"Pine. I cut some pine branches for you. I'll bring it in when my shoes are clean."

She kissed him and smiled. "Pine?"

"You were talking about how your family always decorated the church with pine and whatnot. I thought you might want to do the same here. I hacked down a small tree like the German folks from your father's congregation."

Eleanor looked up at him with glistening eyes. "Yes. I would like that very much."

* * *

"It is Christmas Eve," Eleanor said to her husband as he stood leaning back on the closed door of the cabin. "I would rather not go into town if you do not mind. I've woven the soft pine together to drape on the mantel and must finish cleaning the turkey you shot so that I can roast it for our dinner tomorrow."

"We've both been working very hard with moving in. I'd planned for us to take a meal together in town and there is something I want you to see."

Eleanor looked up at Beau. He was upset or nervous, she wasn't sure which, but only found herself admiring his broad shoulders and thinking of him without a stitch of clothing, crawling in bed with her last night, their first one together in their home. He'd made slow love to her, whispering his intentions in her ear and trailing her neck with feather kisses, as she ran trembling fingers over every part of his body. She woke up that morning wondering where her flannel nightgown had gone and blushed again with the remembrance. Where would she be without his protection? Surely she could turn the lamps up and prepare the turkey when she came home.

She pulled her bonnet from the hook by the door and shrugged into her woolen coat. "Will you read more to me this evening?"

"I will. Your father's store of books will entertain us through a long winter."

The day was crisp and clear, and she leaned on her husband's arm. "What a fine day. I am glad we are taking a holiday together. We *have* both been working very hard."

Beau pulled the wagon into the stables and talked with the stable master, Theodore Wilkins.

"Good day to you and Merry Christmas, Beauregard!"

"And to you, Theodore. I have not introduced my wife to you, have I? This is Mrs. Gentry," Beau said. "Mr. Theodore Wilkins."

"Merry Christmas! Please call me Eleanor," she said and smiled. "It is a pleasure to meet you, sir."

"I've been telling Mrs. Wilkins that there are newlyweds at the old Ferguson cabin. She told me she'd like you to join us for a Sunday dinner when the weather is good."

"That would be wonderful," Eleanor said.

"Whatever makes my bride happy is fine with me," Beau added.

"And you'd best remember that as the years go by," Mr. Wilkins said with a laugh and a slap on Beau's shoulder.

"He is still here, is he not?" he asked Mr. Wilkins.

"Yes, he's here. The man is talking of moving on and taking him to the next town, though. If you want him, I would advise speaking to the man soon."

Beau guided Eleanor to a stall in the back of the stables. "He is a Morgan. A stallion that is a direct descendent of Figure, the original Morgan, through Figure's son, Woodbury."

The horse was huge compared to Bristol or even Nellie, and he stood still looking over Beau and her as if he were crowning them the winners. Eleanor held out a hand, heard Beau's hiss of disapproval and the horse nicker and nudge her fingers.

"You are thinking of buying him?"

"If I can make a deal we can afford and you agree."

"Are you selling him, Mr. Wilkins?"

"No, ma'am. A man came through town a few weeks ago and has been stabling him here and looking for a buyer. He won him in poker game in Philadelphia and is down on his luck. He has the papers to prove the horse is, indeed, a Morgan through Woodbury and has a letter from the Morgan family as well."

"How much is he asking?"

"One-hundred and twenty-five in gold or a hundred in silver," Mr. Wilkins said.

Beau tipped his hat to the stable master, pulled her arm through his, and walked her down the street and up the wooden boards leading to the door of the restaurant near the hotel. It was crowded inside with guests and noisy as customers spoke to each other about Christmas plans at church and home. Eleanor was glad then that Beau had brought her to town. There was a festive atmosphere, full of anticipation and the pleasurable meeting of neighbors and friends. She listened to two young girls asking their mother time and again what special treats she was making for the next day.

"What are you thinking, Eleanor?"

"Those girls remind me of my youngest sister, Ruth," she said softly. "So happy and carefree."

"As I wish you were right now."

"I am happy. Happier than I ever thought I

might be, but that does not mean I am not missing my family." She reached across the table to touch his hand. "But you are my family now and I am yours. Our marriage is a gift I am so lucky to have."

"I'll never replace your mother and father and sisters."

"No. And I realize it will take some time for me to heal. I had been numb to their deaths to some degree, worried about my own survival and how I would carry on. Just lately, I've been thinking about them so much more. Perhaps it is the holiday approaching or that I am so happy, and maybe feeling guilty for being so, but that is not right. The guilt, I mean. My parents and sisters would have never, ever begrudged my survival. Oh, I am feeling emotional and talking too much. What of this horse?"

Beau seemed satisfied to change the subject. "I think if I can get the man down to ninety dollars in silver, we should buy him with your father's money."

"Our silver, Beau. That would take nearly all of it, would it not?"

"Yes. We will have the gold, but it would be lean until we would have a yearling to sell. But I think it will be worth it. With the Morgan name and pedigree, we will be able to get high prices for our horses. Nellie is a Tennessee Walker and I think would breed well. I don't know anything about Bristol."

"Then we will be frugal. Perhaps I can take in sewing or do some other work."

"Are you sure, Eleanor? I don't want to force you into something you do not want to do. It will only cause us problems in the end."

"I am sure. I trust you. And we can never know unseen events that may change things and make our plans work or fail. I trust you to do the best for us."

He smiled, clasped her hands across the table, and kissed both her palms. "This is the start of it, Eleanor. This is the beginning. Remember this day so we can tell our children and grandchildren how we began our empire at Paradise."

He turned to read the clock sitting on the mantel of the room. "We should go. Are you done?"

"Yes, yes, of course. We should be getting back home."

He hurried her out the door, down the planks, and to the portion of the street that was dry.

"The stable is the other way, Beau," she said and hurried to keep up with his long strides.

"There's something I want you to see. There's the train."

Eleanor went up the steps to the train station platform as the whistle blew, Beau at her back. "What could we possibly want to see here?"

"Over there. The passengers are getting off. Straight ahead, Eleanor."

She complied, with little idea why they were there, but weaving nonetheless through the travelers boarding and departing the train. "There are more people coming and going than I would expect," she said and looked up at her husband. He was busy scanning the crowd. "What is this about, Beau?"

"Train only comes down this spur every two weeks. No other stations for a hundred miles, maybe more."

"Beau? Why are we here?"

"Eleanor? Eleanor?" she heard and turned to the crowd of passengers that had just disembarked. She shaded her eyes.

She took in a sharp breath and felt her husband's arm come around her waist. "Aunt Brigid?"

A white-haired woman dropped her bags where she stood and hurried to them. She pulled Eleanor into her arms, stroked and patted her hair, and kissed her cheek.

"It is me, lamb," she said softly. "Cry as much as you wish. Aunt Brigid is here."

Eleanor did not know how long she stood in her aunt's embrace. There was a familiarity that was more than she could parse. The woman looked so very much like her brother and sounded like him, too, that Eleanor would have known her as McManus anywhere. It was as if she were able to hug her father one last time. She dried her eyes on a handkerchief that Beau handed her.

"How did this happen? I thought you were ill."

"I was ill, Eleanor, very ill. It took me months to recover, but I am well. My sickness made me realize how ridiculous your father's and my arguments were. I was planning to visit your family in Allentown when your father said he had accepted the post in Charleston. And then I got your letter. Oh my dearest! To have witnessed what you have! You're a strong girl, Eleanor."

"It was horrible, aunt. All of it."

"And we shall talk at length, but I am getting quite cold. Where is this hotel you told me about, young man? You are her young man, her husband, if I'm not mistaken."

"I am," Beau said and pulled his hat from his head. "Beauregard Gentry, at your service."

Chapter Six

Eleanor's thoughts were in shambles and she would have far preferred to stand right where she was and have her questions answered, but her aunt was cold, as the wind blew across the station platform when the train pulled away, and she was as well. She linked arms with her and led her to the warmth of the hotel lobby.

Aunt Brigid untied the ribbons on her hat and unbuttoned her coat. There was a fire in the potbelly stove and she stood before it, holding her hands out to warm them.

"How did you know how to find me?" Eleanor asked. "I fear the letter I sent you right after my parents died was hardly legible. I was hysterical, I think."

"Of course you were," Brigid said.

"Your aunt's reply arrived by stagecoach on the first of December. I was in the mercantile buying the lamp oil when Mr. Fisher handed me her letter. I didn't give it to you then, I should have, but I wanted to see if I could get her to travel here and surprise you. Her letter to you is unopened back at Paradise. Her address was on the outside of the envelope, and I wrote to her. I paid a man I met at the stables taking the train to Philadelphia to hand deliver my letter to her."

"I received Mr. Gentry's letter and closed my shop up and began making arrangements to travel here to you. I sent him a return letter the following day."

"I got it yesterday, ma'am. I was ever so relieved that you were arriving. Eleanor is grieving sorely and she needs family."

Eleanor felt the tears tumbling off of her cheeks. "Aunt Brigid. They are gone. All of them."

"Yes, dear. I know."

"Can I take you both back to our home, to Paradise? I will bring you back to the hotel this evening. That way you can have privacy to talk," Beau said.

"Yes, please, Beau. Should we arrange a room for you, Aunt Brigid? I am sorry to say we don't have a place for you yet in our cabin."

"It's already arranged," Beau said. "I'll tell the clerk to put her bags in her room."

* * *

"After all is said and done, Eleanor, there is no one for me in my little town any longer, and why would I not want to be near my brother's daughter? I can sew clothing in any town. Why not Winchester?"

"You would close up your shop?" Eleanor asked as she turned from the fireplace to serve her aunt a cup of tea. "Father said you were very successful making clothing for the wealthy women of Philadelphia."

"Not every year has been profitable, but most have. My assistant wants to buy the store and has relatives willing to lend her the money. She has earned it, to my thinking, having put up with me for the last fifteen years. She is capable and will do well, I think. Fresh ideas will be welcome. What do you think?"

Eleanor cried then, in earnest. "I have felt very alone, even though Beau has been all I could ask for in a husband and more. I love him. I am certain of it. But I grew up with my sisters and Mother and Father and a large church family. I would be very pleased if you were here, near us. Beau has great plans for our property and future.

I would want you to be part of it."

"Then your husband will have to make inquiries for me for a storefront with living quarters above on one of the main streets. I will plan on spring to be here permanently."

Eleanor clasped her aunt's hands. "I am so happy. What a wonderful Christmas present you have been."

Beau took Aunt Brigid to town to the hotel near sunset and returned cold and weary after dark.

"I have torn myself up inside, knowing that I withheld a letter from you. It was wrong of me."

Eleanor walked to him where he stood at the mantel, poking and prodding the fire to life and staring at the flames. She put her arms around his waist. "You are high-handed sometimes; I can already tell that about you. That does not mean I am not grateful for everything you have done for me, and I know whatever you have done was to make me feel better, to comfort me. There is no one in this world I would rather be beside than you. I love you, Beauregard Gentry."

"I love you, too, Eleanor."

* * *

A brisk wind was blowing and swirling dry snow when Eleanor and Beau arrived at the hotel to pick up Aunt Brigid for Christmas church service the following morning. He had worn his best shirt, one of three he owned and the same one he'd worn the day they'd married. His hair was slicked back, and he'd scraped every bit of mud he could from his boots. Both women were dressed fancy and fine, just like Aunt Dorthea on Christmas Day. He drove them the few blocks to the church and climbed down from the wagon to help them down and to the church doors.

Eleanor kissed his cheek. "Thank you for bringing us. It will be an hour or more, I imagine. Where will you be?"

"I'll be out front waiting."

Eleanor and her aunt turned to the church and waited with many other townsfolk in line to greet that nitwit Buckland, all wrapped up in his self-righteous glory, shaking hands with the men and inviting the women inside. Beau's wife and her aunt were already making new acquaintances with the family ahead of them. He stood and watched the procession as he leaned against the wagon where he'd parked it across the street. He hand-fed Bristol and laid a wool blanket over her and Nellie as they'd both worked up a sweat and now stood in the cold air. He supposed he could take the wagon to the stable. Theodore wouldn't care if he got his animals out of the wind.

But he didn't. Beau was watching his wife nod, shake hands, and hold some woman's infant while the other attended a small child. His wife looked fine holding a baby. A tall man came down the street toward him then, and Beau wondered who he was and where he came from as he'd just seemed to appear from between the two buildings Beau was sheltering beside. The man walked up to him, smiled, and laid a hand on his shoulder. It was odd, Beau thought at the time and after, that it didn't bother him in the least that a stranger was touching him.

"Merry Christmas," the man said. "You are Beauregard, are you not?"

Beau tilted his head. "Yes, I am. You have me at a disadvantage, sir. I do not know your name."

The tall man smiled. "I see you looking at your bride. She is the one there in the green and red silk with her aunt beside her. She is a beautiful young woman."

Beau looked at Eleanor, at her smile, heard her laugh, watched as she touched the head of a small child. "Eleanor's beauty lies within, although I consider her the loveliest woman I've ever met. There is no woman braver than she. I am in awe of her."

"Then why do you stand here, son? Why are you not with her?"

Beau looked down at the ground as he moved a stone back and forth with the toe of his boot. "There's a man in there that wanted her first. He wasn't good enough for her, but he was one of her kind. I've drifted around and done some things, some killing even, that makes me *not* one of her kind."

"The killing you've done saved her life, did it not?"

"Yes, it did," he said, and wondered how much of Eleanor's story had been told around town. He hated to see her be the subject of gossip. Yet, who knew those details except he and Eleanor?

"Do you love her?"

Beau looked at his wife, now shaking hands with Reverend Buckland. "Yes. With all my strength and being."

"Then go to her. Hear the Savior's story and the sacred music beside her. Be brave, Beauregard, as your wife is brave. She loves you above all others."

He turned and looked at the man. He was familiar, yet Beau was certain he'd never met him. What was it about him that compelled him to do just what the man had said? To go to Eleanor and begin new memories for her, new Christmas memories, new traditions that they would share with her aunt and their children yet to be born.

"I will do just that," Beau said as the man walked away. "Happy Christmas to you."

The tall man turned. "Love them both, Beauregard. Keep Christ in your heart and guard Brigid and my dear Eleanor."

"I promise," he said.

The church bells pealed at that moment and Beau looked at the steeple. *Brigid? His dear Eleanor?* He turned quickly but the man was nowhere to be seen up or down the street or even in the alley behind him. He had vanished.

Beau hurried up the stone steps of the church and opened the heavy ornate door. He walked down the center aisle, hat in hand, looking for his wife, and found her near the front of the church. He slipped into the seat beside her, smelling the pine draped on the altar and the wax polish used on the oak pews. She looked up at him and smiled.

"Beauregard," she whispered. "I am so glad you came inside. What changed your mind, husband?"

He covered her hand where it held her hymnal. "I made a promise which I will keep forever and a day. Merry Christmas, Eleanor," he said and kissed her.

Thank you for your purchase of *Into the Evermore*. Eleanor and Beauregard raise three children at Paradise and Matthew Gentry's story will release in the spring of 2017.

Please stop by my website, hollybushbooks.com, to read samples of all my American Historical romances including The Crawford Family Series – *Train Station Bride, Contract to Wed,* and *Her Safe Harbor*, and standalones *Romancing Olive* and *Reconstructing Jackson*. *Cross the Ocean* and *Charming the Duke* are both British Victorian historical romances.

I announce new releases and other book news on my Facebook page, my Amazon Author page, and my BookBub page. I'd love for you to stop by!

The first few pages of Matthew Gentry's story are below.

For more information or to contact me:
Twitter: @hollybushbooks
Facebook: hollybushbooks
www.hollybushbooks.com
holly@hollybushbooks.com

EXCERPT

Chapter One

1869 Outskirts of Lexington, Kentucky

"Don't pinch, Esmie! It hurts!"

The blond woman propped against the foot of the metal bed giggled and fondled her own breast. She glanced at the man lounging against the headboard and ran the tip of her tongue around her lips. "Tillie seems put out, sweetheart. Why don't you and me have some fun?"

"I like to have fun, too, Esmie. I'll play," the redhead lying on her side next to the man said.

Matt Gentry took another swig of whiskey from the bottle in his left hand. He was drunk, but not so far gone that he couldn't enjoy himself with the two naked women in his bed, but it had been a day or so, he thought, since he'd done much of anything but drink his rye and screw. He was almost tired of it. Almost.

Esmie crawled to him, eyes on him, and began to kiss and lick his bare leg. He leaned back against the pillows and gave a hum of contentment as Esmie found other things to run her tongue over. Not to be outdone, Tillie crouched near him, swinging one enormous breast in front of his face as she did. He sucked her nipple until it stood straight and hard. His hips were starting to pump when the door to his hotel room flew open.

Matt's right hand shot up, aiming a six-shooter at the man in doorway, and he disengaged himself from Tillie's breast to take a look-see at who he was pointing his gun at. "Ben? Is that you?" he asked.

"Who else would it be?"

Matt shook his head and started to laugh. "Who else would it be? Ha! How about that, girls? Who else would it be?"

Ben Littleship, the ranch manager for Paradise, his family's spread in Virginia for as long as Matt could remember, was staring at him. Ben was as stone-faced as a man could be, but even Matt in his stupor and having been away from home for well on eight years could tell he was disgusted with what he saw. Matt pushed Esmie away and sat up. The room tilted even though he had two feet on the floor. "Go on girls. Get some clothes on and take a walk."

"We could entertain ourselves, honey," Esmie said and winked at Ben Littleship, "and your new friend, too."

"Does he owe you any money?" Ben asked the two women.

"He pays us good but we'd do it for free," Tillie said.

"Go on," Matt said. "Time for a break."

The two women walked around the bed and to the door. Ben held out a coin as they went by. "Have a pot of coffee and two meals sent up. Right quick."

Esmie took the coin, bit down on it, and dropped it in the pocket of the silky robe she wore. "Sure thing, honey."

Ben sat down in the one chair in the room, a dainty velvet-covered item, and looked out the window of the second-floor room.

Matt pulled on his pants and ran a hand over the stubble of his beard. His hair was dark red, nearly brown, just like his mother's, and he was as powerfully built as his father with a broad chest and thick arms. He rubbed at his left shoulder where a horse had kicked him years ago.

"What are you doing here, Ben?" Matt waited while the old man casually watched the passersby on the street below. "Are you going to tell me why you're here?"

"Eat first."

"Mother send you? She worried the devil in me finally won? Sure as hell wasn't Daddy that sent you, that's for damn certain."

Ben turned his head to stare at him. The two men were quiet together for nearly a quarter of an hour.

Tillie opened the door and let in a young boy carrying a tray of food and an older woman behind him carrying coffee and tin mugs. Tillie winked at him, and he could see Esmie over her shoulder, smiling wickedly. The two women suddenly looked cheap and sordid, but he imagined he looked the same to them. A young drunk with plenty of money, little judgment, and a reckless glint in his eye. Ah . . . what had he become?

The woman and boy left the room and Matt shooed the two women out the door. He eyed the beefsteak and fried potatoes and burped. He filled a mug with coffee, hoping Ben did not see his hands shaking as too much liquor, too little sleep, and no real food he could remember had taken their toll.

Ben pulled a plate from the tray and sat it

on the table beside him. He opened the napkin, shook it, and laid it across his lap. He cut the meat into small pieces, speared a potato, and ate. Matt found himself staring at the ranch manager as if he'd never been taught any fine manners or courtesies and did not know what to make of the behavior of a gentleman. Matt went to the washstand, lathered up his hands with the scented soap beside the bowl, washed his face and arms, and rinsed out his mouth, gargling with the warm water and nearly gagging. He combed back his hair and tied it with a piece of rawhide.

Matt dragged a second chair to the small table, thinking the food smells were appetizing now, more than the aroma of coffee or the stench of the booze on his clothes. He ate in small bites and chewed slowly, not trusting his stomach to manage a large or quick meal. The food and coffee cleared his head, leaving him to wonder what the ranch manager was doing here. He looked up from his plate now, searching the face of the man staring at him with an unrelenting gaze. A shiver trailed down his arms, a ghost or a memory, flitting over him and leaving him with the sure knowledge that there was bad news coming.

Matt wiped his mouth with his napkin and laid it on the table. "What is it? What has happened?"

"Your father's dead. Almost a month now."

Made in the USA
Columbia, SC
04 June 2018